FRACTURED REVOLUTION

by Leigh Maris

FRACTURED REVOLUTION

LEIGH MARIS

Splintered Orchard
Press

SYNOPSIS

Jamie Harken is about to turn sixteen. His world is also about to change forever. His brother, Hogan, and the world around the Harken family are obsessed with the evolution of artificial intelligence. Renowned technology company Ovvl is about to push this evolving society over the edge. There will be fracturing. Everyone will have to make choices. And Jamie will question what the line is between hope and fear.

Jamie Harken is fifteen years and eleven months old when the world as he knows it begins to fracture.

Jamie's foot presses gently on the gas pedal of his father's Ford F150. His hands rest at ten and two, the way his father taught him only a few months ago, and he coaxes the vehicle out of the vacant lot three exits away from their neighborhood. Jamie's dad, Lance, sits beside him in the passenger seat. Jamie's driver's exam is a month away, so he's insisted on having his dad take him out driving as often as they can this summer. Muscle memory is something Jamie's heard to be helpful in routine matters like this. Not that many of his peers would know. Several of them don't practice driving automatic cars since their parents keep only self-driving cars in the garage. *Quite silly, frankly, to call non-self-driving cars "automatic,"* Jamie thinks. *True automation is self-driving. How lacking in imagination our ancestors were.* Jamie's family is part of the slowly decreasing majority of folks that don't have any such smart vehicles. Not that Lance would ever acknowledge the people around the Harken family are slowly changing their ways, slowly becoming less tactile, slowly accepting the convenience and comfort of the technology at their disposal. Slowly evolving.

"Good work, son. Nice and steady on the gas," says Lance from his seat beside Jamie. Lance shakes his head, as he frequently does on these test drives. But Jamie knows not to become disheartened by his father's movements. Jamie knows his father's faith in him is stronger than his faith in Jamie's generation. "You're learning a skill soon few will remember."

Lance is always saying what a weird time this is. And sometimes Jamie supposes he is right. The whole reason he is here driving his father's old F150 with its tires all controlled by an axle connected to a wheel that Jamie himself maneuvers is because the United States is split on the matter of artificial intelligence. Some folks can't wait to see the day planes are self-flying, and some folks would rather stick to human pilots and human air traffic controllers over the virtual air traffic controllers that the larger airports are starting to roll out.

On the whole, their society is locked in a debate. When is relying on AI acceptable?

When does efficiency rule out self-sufficiency?

In the instance of commuter vehicles, however, the efficient side won. The United States will phase out manual-drive and automatic cars in favor of self-driving cars the same way cashiers were phased out of grocery stores and store managers were replaced with intelligent surveillance to catch and track shoplifters lifting Tall Boys out of freezers in unpatrolled liquor aisles. The phase out date is already set. His older brother, Hogan, tells him this is the future. *Get over it already*.

Jamie is likely to get over it. His generation is this mid-century one. He was born into the evolving world. But he knows someone who will hold a decades long grudge. Centuries long even if science comes to allow it. Lance.

His father has always been a bit of a luddite, which is why Jamie is cruising out of this vacant lot in perhaps the most old-school American truck known to man. A 2000 Ford F150. It's painted white and has only two seats. The truck bed is durable but scuffed from years of his father throwing various pieces of furniture in it from moves across town and purchasing items beloved mostly by old men (like their spartan lawnmower with zero wireless audio streaming capability). His father's receipts litter the floor on the passenger side, something the youth, familiar only with email receipts, would know nothing about. There's not even a touch screen GPS-radio inside.

But the phase-out date for manual-drive and automatic cars is coming. The government, automobile resellers, and private sector manufacturers announced it two years ago: January 1, 2085. All manual-drive and automatic cars will be recalled and recycled by that date. The advances of the mid-century will inevitably overtake the old traditions. Lance will have to return his beloved daily drive to the authorities. Or, really, just trade it in for a self-driving vehicle. One more reason for him to hate this new generation. And, in ten years' time, the North American electric vehicle charging network should be preeminent. His father's generation will just have to learn.

But for the time being, Jamie is the one who has to learn how to drive. He's not at liberty to simply learn voice commands and nonverbal cues like some of his peers. His family won't be purchasing a self-driving car any time soon. Even with a mother as technologically savvy as his own.

Next to him, his father scratches his unkempt beard as if to wipe the scowl off his face. As if to remind himself that he is doing his part to teach his son what he's learned and pass down the skills that once set him free. He rests one arm on the center console and one arm on the window arm rest. His forearms are bare, which is a state Jamie still isn't used to seeing them in after years of his father wearing button downs. Instead, Lance wears a T-shirt, blue jeans, and an old college cap. A pair of black framed prescription glasses rest on the bridge of his nose. His eyesight is shot from years of looking closely at figures all day. This new outfit of T-shirts and blue jeans quickly became his father's brand when his employer let him go three months ago. He used to be a bookkeeper. But automated software has now completely replaced his role.

Jamie reaches out and turns the radio dial from the classical music station to news. His father insists that during their lessons they play classical music. "Helps with your focus, son. And simulates slight distraction. No sane person drives in silence every car ride of their life." Jamie returns his hands to the wheel so they assume that 10 and 2 position again. His father isn't really talking at this point. He used his voice in the parking lot only when he needed to. And he will use his voice on this ride home only when he needs to. His father is quite practical like that. He always has been - not only since three months ago.

"Today is Sunday, June 2, 2030, and you're listening to FM 98.8." The truck's speakers rumble along with its engine. "Today, the Artificial Intelligence Regulatory Board approved Ovvl's plan to release its long-awaited Brain Computer Interface to the public. Previously, BCI technology has been reserved only for private use by the researchers studying 500 participants across the nation to determine the technology's long-term viability. With its twenty-year research period concluded, and results and side effects reviewed by the AIRB, Ovvl has been granted a license to sell directly to consumers and provide invasive brain surgery to install their devices at licensed and regulated clinics across the US.

For those still unfamiliar with BCIs, they are small, disc shaped devices that can be implanted in the brain to directly communicate the brain's electrical activity with external devices, most commonly computers or robotic limbs, thus effectively skipping intermediary body parts like the hands, feet, and head. BCIs have been a coveted tool among the rehabilitative, prosthetic, and disability treatment industries since the 1970s, although this is the first time in history a BCI will be available for purchase by the public. Critics worry about the erasure of the distinction between brain and machine, although, I would really love if I could wake up in the morning, *think* about making coffee, and walk into my kitchen to a freshly brewed pot waiting for me courtesy *a la* BCI. Clare, our bodies are *really* evolving."

"Public consumption?" His father's eyes sharpen. Were Jamie monitoring his father's pulse, Jamie is certain he would have detected a spike. His father only speaks when he needs to. And his father always needs answers when he asks. He is no rhetorical questions kind of man. No practical reason for those, Lance says.

"Yep, I heard that too," Jamie acknowledges his father and tries to keep his eyes on the road as he listens to Lance's weight shift around in the passenger seat. Lance must be trying to get comfortable after hearing such unsettling news. "Hogan's going to want one." The radio continues quacking in the background. Jamie checks his rearview mirror and side mirror before merging to the right. Their exit is coming up. Jamie sees, briefly, his father cross his arms and legs when he glances in the side mirror. He is certain

Lance's right hand his also placed between his lips and under his chin like it always is when he is in thought or feeling particularly critical. Often, Jamie finds his father like this while sitting at his desk pouring over receipts and combing through journal entries. Or he used to at least.

"Oh but will your mom and I let him get one is the question."

"Ovvl plans to release the product next Monday, although pre-order is available as soon as today. Up next is the daily market report. Phat AI is up 60 percentage points and the global Brain Computer Interface and Body Modification Industry is seeing an upswing following the AIRB's approval of Ovvl's BCI release." *Nonchalant.* Nonchalant would be the word Jamie would use to describe the radio host's voice.

Much less nonchalant is his father's. "Can you believe that barbaric technology has the government's blessing to be offered to the public now?" He waits for Jamie's response. "Exit 12, by the way, son." *I knew that,* Jamie bites his tongue and turns his blinker on to merge right once again. Then he weighs in his mind whether he saw the BCI release coming. If there is anything his father taught him, it was to pause to consider his own thoughts before responding. *A half-baked response can hurt you worse than salmonella,* was one of Lance's strange sayings that made no sense at all to Jamie. He tries not to let unpuzzling his father's sayings keep him up at night.

"Of course. The human trials have been going on for over a decade now, Dad. I heard Ovvl released like 20,000 updates for those participants over the span of the trial too. The tech has gotten better everywhere. I mean, even Sandusky, Ohio has delivery pizza drones now. We won't have manual-drive cars much longer." He tries not to roll his eyes at his father. He tries to remind himself his father simply grew up in a much more primitive generation. "And barbaric is rich, Dad. I think even Mom would agree that the generation you guys grew up in was much more *barbaric* than this one." Jamie takes Exit 12 and leaves the highway behind them. He checks the rearview mirror and side mirror again. In doing so, he catches Jaime's eyes rolling and his mouth lurch to the side in a pout. Jamie turns on his blinker and pulls over to the left to make the next turn.

"Guess so," says Lance. He sits there a while not speaking. No need to speak if he doesn't have anything to say. Then he shifts his weight again, uncrossing his arms and legs. "Strange thing it is, Jamie. Hearing how typical these really atypical things are from your own son's mouth. You may have half my DNA but we certainly are from two separate generations." Jamie realizes his grip on the steering wheel had tightened. They had been driving on the same road for about a mile now. The turn into their borough is coming up. "Yet you give me perspective. Even if I hate what the reality of it means." Jamie loosens his grip on the wheel and puts his blinker on again. To his father's credit, Lance is a tactile man in a nearly virtual world. Because of this, he has some major issues with Jamie's generation and the world they are all entering into.

Jamie and his father pull into their short driveway. The neighborhood around them is quiet except for the sounds of suburban office workers walking their dogs on their lunch breaks. Occasionally, one of them calls their dog's name. "Tesla! Come here." Most of the middle-class work from home these days. Many of the neighbors wear Treads, the popular athleisure brand of the year that pioneered the orthopedic Tread Number and adjustable memory foam insoles with temperature control. The technology adjusts the incline and bevel of your shoes and, of course, the temperature, of your lower extremities. All while tracking your steps and investing a fixed value for every 1,000 steps earned. The children out of school on summer break are all indoors on virtualverse chat rooms with their friends.

As Jamie and his father walk through the doorway of their home, Jamie notices his father glance at the video doorbell fixed to the brick wall outside. Their family's decision to put a video doorbell outside of their home was a huge domestic conflict. His mother thought it was the natural next step for total home security. Jamie and his brother, Hogan, thought of the video doorbell as a doorman, like all of their peers did. They fondly named him David. But their father thought the addition was a bit capitalist-security-state-ish and insisted a doorman was a man who stood outside a door and not a video camera made of metals and plastics. "How can a piece of glass and wiring, not immune to destruction mind you, protect us better than an expert who can run to your aid and knows self-defense? And how valuable are overheard conversations to these monolithic corporations?" Hogan and Jamie chuckled at this. It sounded to them like his father was referring to the bouncers they had seen in movies protecting 21+ dance clubs and not a doorman protecting an apartment from unknown guests, like in the dramedy series set in New York their mother liked to watch every now and then.

"Honey, it's a tool that gives us information we wouldn't have otherwise. If there's some strange bump in the night, I am not going to pull back a curtain to get a good visual. I'd rather pull up footage on my phone in a room twenty feet away and call the police." His mother knew his father needed answers when he asked questions. And the morning after she gave this answer, a video doorbell was installed on the brick wall outside. The feud was called off.

Jamie and his brother still call it Doorman David. Whenever their family orders pizza delivery, and the motion of the delivery drone sets off the video doorbell's motion sensors, the two announce that Doorman David has their pizza hot and ready. Lance hates this. "*Not* what a doorman is, sons." Technically, Jamie thought, there wasn't much difference. The video feed routes to a man who has a clear view of the world outside the door. A doorman was a man whose eyes had a clear view of the world outside the door. A man or a video feed, what was the big difference when their pizza ended up at the right doorstep every time?

All this time, Jamie looks forward to July 2nd. The date of his driver's exam fills him with more excitement than his sixteenth birthday itself, which is the day before. "Jamie, you should take your exam the day after your birthday – that way, when you pass, you get an extra day of celebration," his mother suggested to him with her gentle smile.

"Yeah, or at least you won't ruin your birthday if you fail!" said Hogan.

Jamie looks forward to proving Hogan wrong, although the potential of failing the exam is yet another reason he's been so insistent on taking lessons with his father. If he passes on the first go, he can drive himself to school when it starts in the fall. Junior year of high school will be much more liberating with four wheels. Virtual reality can only take you so far. And his father doesn't like Jamie and Hogan using virtual reality headsets in their house anyway. He's arranged a time limit to kick him and Hogan out after some period of time that Lance has decided is "far too many hours of use." July 2nd is only two weeks away. Which means, hopefully soon, Jamie will be able to drive to some virtual reality cafe when his hours of use time out.

He lays on his bed staring up at the ceiling. As much as his intent is to frequent virtual reality cafes when he gets his driver's license, Jamie loves living inside moments of stillness. Small habits like this come out in Jamie sometimes – habits much like those of his father. Lance too, has a habit of sitting in moments of stillness. Or perhaps both, rather, have habits of being still in moments of the world stirring. Jamie's favorite spot for these moments is atop his comforter. Lance's favorite spot for these moments is atop his recliner – usually around nine or ten in the evening.

Sun floods into Jamie's room through the window by his bed. He doesn't have traditional curtains like in the movies. He has voice commanded blinds, courtesy of his mother who loves to ask their virtual assistant, Paul, to pull up the blinds and get her sons out of their bat caves. She did that earlier today, and now Jamie watches the summer sunlight dance across his walls and ceiling. The calm nothingness of this moment reminds Jamie of summers from his youth, before he was allowed to have electronics in his room. Before he was allowed to have electronics on his wrist and face. He covets the summers from his youth like he covets the electronics built into their house. Neither is better or worse to Jamie.

He sees it simply as the evolution of time and growing up.

He reaches his arm out toward his bedside table and swipes his smart glasses off their cradle. They were a gift from his fourteenth birthday. He'd taken good care of them the last two years. The glasses, which he routinely caresses with a microfiber cloth, have not once fractured from clumsy misuse or being stepped on.

Hogan broke his own pair two months in to owning them. Jamie remembers how Hogan had to pick up a job at the local drive-up burger joint to pay for their replacement. Hogan always bragged about the tips he made. "I'm telling you, bro. The suggested tip bubbles our tablets display at the end of a greasy meal always get us a little something sweet. Nobody carries cash anymore. Not that we have the equipment to accept it anyway. Sure, tips are taxed this way, but we make way more dough than we used to from tips. The computer doing the math for the customer really helps. People usually look at the percentages rather than the dollar amounts too. Way better than when we used to run our laughable lemonade stands, Jamie." When he finally saved up enough digits in his online savings account, Hogan bought an upgraded pair. His new smart glasses were a newer generation than Jamie's, and Jamie noticed. Hogan always liked *new*. *Hedonic Hogan would make a good nickname,* Jamie sometimes thought.

Jamie places his smart glasses on his face and uses the buttons and dials on his watch to control the screen the glasses project. He needs to study, but he is feeling far too lazy and stuck in a summer haze to be bothered to sit at a desk. Instead, Jamie presses the button on the side of his wristwatch and projects an internet tab through his glasses. He pauses for a moment. If he ever got a BCI himself, he wouldn't even need to press the button on the side of his wristwatch to browse his glasses. He searches for the latest driver's exam questions and pulls up a lengthy mock exam before him. He needs to study these questions and answers because there will be a written portion as well as a driving portion. He also heard the Department of Motor and Electric Vehicles was beginning to focus more heavily on electric and self-driving car questions, which he knows very little about.

How do you tell a self-driving car to go to a new destination?

A.   *Give it a voice command.*

B.   Type the destination name into its intelligent dashboard.

C.   Put the car in manual drive and ask it to record the new route.

Well, not C unless you're maybe my father, Jamie thinks. *Giving a voice command seems far too obvious an answer to be the right one. I'm sure these test makers are trying to trick us. Perhaps a voice command wouldn't make sense if it's a* new *destination. Right? You wouldn't have assigned a voice command to a new location yet. But maybe it means that we should assign voice commands to all new destinations?* Jamie's head hurt from looking at some of these questions. His finger hovers over option B. Finally, he selects option A. Jamie's vision flashes red. Or rather, the projected screen flashes red and the exam selects option B in red text. *So option B was the right answer. So close.* The webpage explains that new locations don't have voice commands pre-programmed. The new destination must be typed in and a voice command programmed first. Jamie supposes he might have a reason to fear this driver's exam after all.

_____ is to putting a self-driving car in reverse as _____ is to putting an automatic car in reverse?

A.   Saying "Reverse"; Checking your seatbelt.

B.   Saying "Reverse"; Pushing "R."

C.   Doing nothing; Slowly easing on the gas.

Some of these exam questions make Jamie think of his sophomore year English teacher, Ms. Hart. English exams are keen on asking questions like this. Nearly any of these could be the answer but two are supposed to obviously be wrong if you know the mathematics of words. Jamie sighs. *Option C seems a good bet because everyone knows truly self-driving cars require no human assistance. But then, option C clearly neglects a direction in which you're to ease onto the gas.* Jamie taps his fingers against the side of his left leg. *Think, Jamie.* He lifts his hand to his face and brushes his dark black hair away from his forehead. This exam has him sweating the advances of the mid-century world as much as constructing train tracks had rail workers sweating. *Okay, so option A and option B for self-driving cars are basically equivalent. Alright, then it comes down to whether one ought to check *their seatbelt or push the R gear in an automatic car.* Jamie purses his lips. *Well this one is actually easy.* He presses option B. Jamie's vision flashes green and the exam selects option B in green text. Jamie sighs with relief.

Just then, there is a loud noise – a door slamming downstairs. Surely, it's Hogan. Jamie peers out his bedroom window, which is situated over their garage and overlooks their front yard. He watches Hogan jog away from their house and hop into one of his friend's rides. Jamie sees his brother slap hands with another high school senior who starts talking with him and gesticulating with his hands. The car drives them away, letting them keep eye contact with each other and break it whenever one of them needs to roll their eyes. In this moment, Jamie feels a bit of envy rise inside. Hogan, being two years older, gets so much more freedom to do as he pleases. What it must feel like to leave and go wherever you want whenever you want, Jamie can only dream of. He's far away from eighteen, but at least he'll be sixteen soon enough.

Jamie places the smart glasses back down in their cradle. He will study more tomorrow. Perhaps, he can persuade Hogan to let him drive shotgun in one of his friends' self-driving cars. Just to see what the whole thing is about and to better place the concepts he'd read. Two more weeks.

Jamie's mind starts to wander. The girls he went to school with had banquets for their sixteenth birthdays. Real formal, almost ball-type events. And the girls who had their birthdays in the summer always hosted their parties in the virtualverse so anyone could attend, even if they were on vacation with their families. This option was also budget friendly; one could splurge on a cheaper dress for one's virtual avatar than for oneself. Jamie wonders whether he can persuade his father to give him extra virtualverse time on his birthday to throw a virtualverse bash. But, in the moment he considers it, he decides he'd rather play games in the virtualverse than stand around in some ballroom in a virtual tuxedo chatting. All Jamie wants, really, is a birthday tradition. The men in Jamie's family had no sixteenth birthday traditions. Save for, perhaps, individuating.

Later that evening, Lance finds his way to his recliner in the living room. He sits and reclines and loses himself inside his own world.

As much as one is their own person, one is also bits of the people who make them.

Hogan isn't a recluse but he sure feels that way to his family. He always secludes himself from them; instead, choosing the company of friends nobody in his family had ever met or heard of. When he is home, he is always shut away in his room listening to interviews with the volume on high. The interviews always seem to be of some young fortune 2,000 company executive on the brink of either breaking into the mainstream with a brilliant new patent or fighting some lawsuit whereby they were named defendant charged with causes of action like fraud. The interviewees seem far separated from the society in which they live, their view of reality far more distorted than even Lance's view of reality, but Hogan doesn't seem to notice oddities in what they say. The family mostly lets him be himself. Or by himself. But his mother, Deanna, takes issue with Hogan's occasional absenteeism from school and apparent lack of hobbies. Not that she's home enough to confront him about it.

Deanna works a lot. Seeing as his father had been out of work for some three months, an unfortunate consequence of technology's advance, she took on more hours. And there is no shortage of hours a computer scientist can take on in the day and age of smart computers.

Yet, on the afternoon before Jamie's sixteenth birthday, Hogan and Deanna find themselves at home at the same time. This June afternoon has been a hot one. Jamie and Hogan used to kick it on the couch in their living room on hot, summer afternoons like this eating popsicles and pestering the neighborhood kids in the virtualverse treehouse. They made their avatars resemble trolls. But lately, Hogan hadn't wanted to do anything with Jamie, and Jamie is starting to have a serious case of youngest child syndrome. He wants to hang out with Hogan and do as he does. So he walks up the stairs to Hogan's room. When he is within nine feet of Hogan's room, he hears a loud voice coming from the speakers within.

"...and this is a choice mid-century teens are going to have to make for themselves as they near adulthood. Is their future one with AI in it or one without it? Are these young adults willing to pass up lucrative careers and comfortable lifestyles solely because Mommy and Daddy said this reminds them too much of the dystopian movies, or books rather, they grew up with?"

Jamie makes his way closer to Hogan's slightly ajar bedroom door. He reaches it and catches a glimpse of his brother with his backpack disheveled, clothing and toiletries sticking out, and socks littering the floor. *Is he packing?* Jamie pushes the thought from his mind and considers doing what he came upstairs to do – knock on Hogan's door. He hesitates.

"Well, to that, we say AI or Bye! We all know Brain Computer Interfaces change the game. How convenient to have such powerful resources *closer* than at your fingertips? The world as we know it is changing – it's evolving! Human error will be less prevalent, the accuracy of our tools and decisions will increase, our improved efficiency will blow us away, and everyone will start getting these implants. Hey, your wife might disagree, but this type of implant is an even better investment than breast implants! *Not* to participate and proceed living *without* a BCI would be a danger. Who do you think employers are going to hire if they have a choice between an experienced, well-educated person *without* a BCI and an experienced, well-educated person *with* a BCI? Who do you think they'll find more efficient? Who do you think will increase their revenues most? We know exactly who they'd pick. And that's one more reason to say AI or Bye!" Hogan continues shuffling around inside his room. Jamie hears a phone dial tone coming from within.

"Joe, hey. Brad Rayne's got some new info on his website about Upgrowth Cities. Give me a call when you get this."

Jamie feels heat at the back of his throat and at the tips of his hands. His feet draw him backward, downstairs to the living room. He won't be reaching Hogan for a game today. *There's got to be someone searching the virtualverse for company right now. I'll play with them instead.*

Deanna, sick of working in an overheated office and looking forward to baking a sixteenth birthday cake for her youngest son, walks into the house after a commute home from headquarters. The noise of recorded conversation escapes from Hogan's room and wafts down the stairs. She walks into the kitchen and asks Paul to set the oven to 350 degrees.

Jamie is in the living room playing chess with a teenage boy somewhere in Egypt. He is really good at chess, this teenage boy Jamie is playing. Jamie's attention is absorbed by potential counters. The world around him disappears. The world around Jamie sometimes disappears even when he isn't in virtual reality, even when he's looking directly at a puzzle in real time. But this problem of dissociation only worsens when Jamie plays chess in virtual chess rooms. Jamie is in a large ballroom with a small card table in the middle, the square kind that pops open and closed and can be carried just about anywhere. He sees his intellectual opponent sitting opposite him. His opponent's face is composed of pixels but is still a unique avatar with a birthmark on his left cheek and unkempt, dark brown hair that he tucks behind his ears after each move. Jamie almost thinks this is his opponent's tell but realizes his opponent simply programmed the mannerism and probably hoped it would distract whoever was sitting across the table from him from around the world.

Jamie doesn't hear his mother's footsteps on the vinyl floor behind him and jumps when she puts a hand on his shoulder. She squeezes his shoulder once. "Hi, Jamie. Where's your brother?" Jamie pulls the goggles from his face and the ballroom disappears and is replaced by the sight of his mother and the kitchen behind her. He relaxes at her voice and is relieved he hadn't squealed when she squeezed his shoulder. How mortifying it would have been had his opponent heard that. What if he had thought it was related to his move from h1 to h4?

"Beats me if I know," Jamie says. His mother looks around the room, obviously aware Hogan is nowhere in it. Jamie doesn't expect his mother thinks she could find him there, hiding under the table or in the refrigerator. Perhaps that whole room scanning thing is simply something mothers do. Take stock of a room to identify the clues leading them to the whereabouts of their mischievous children.

"I'll bet he's upstairs listening to that nonsense of his," she says. "You know, I worry he's involved in some sort of new age cult." She slips her handbag off her shoulder and takes off her Treads. "What's your read on that?"

"Beats me if I know," Jamie repeats, although he'd be lying if said he hadn't wondered the same. And the words of the man Hogan was listening to creep up over the edge of Jamie's mind: *AI or Bye.*

"You know, he's just never home these days. And not because he's dedicated to a hobby or some band in one of his friend's garages, and he is always listening to some video by that software tycoon Brad Rayne, and whenever he does speak, it's like he's speaking some other language." She pauses. "Then again, maybe that's simply what it's like to be a mom. You kids, and your vernacular. So unlike your parent's generation." She walks to the staircase and begins her ascent.

Jamie turns back to his game of chess but hears Hogan shout when Deanna opens his bedroom door. "Mom, get out!" And she clearly doesn't get out because Hogan's shouting continues. "Please respect my privacy, Mom! A closed door means knock! You taught me that!" Jamie imagines the scene upstairs. He imagines his mother has her hand placed firmly on her hip. Her feet are shoulder width apart. She's staring at Hogan, and he's staring right back at her. He goes to escort her out the door, but she stands firmly planted on the carpet. His clothes are probably strewn about because, as much as he considers himself a responsible young adult, he isn't fully one yet. And then Jamie hears his mother say that.

"Hogan, your room is a mess. Why don't you take some time away from your screen to tidy up?"

"Oh my god, Mom. Get off my case. I'll clean up when I clean up."

"I bet Brad Rayne doesn't leave his clothes all over the floor."

"Yeah, probably not. He sleeps in his garage where he's constantly inventing in the same clothes he's worn for the past three days." Jamie listens to a heavy drawl of silence. Deanna must be locating her patience and trying to figure out this eldest child of hers. Jamie imagines Hogan turns his back to the clothes all over his floor and sits back down at his desk. Of course, he can't actually see what's unraveling upstairs from his perch on the couch in the living room. Funny how we think we know everything about our siblings from growing up with them, but the reality is they have their own story to tell and their own relationships with the same parents and their own inner monologue that you might get really good glimpses into but never hear for yourself. Jamie's new opponent in Brussels moves to e4.

"I'll bet even Brad Rayne cleans his desk. Hard to do all that innovating with too little workspace." His mother says before Jamie hears the conversation die out. He hears light footsteps move across the ceiling from Hogan's room to his parents'. His mother must have decided there are better battles to be fought.

"**S**o, you just turned sixteen yesterday?" Jamie is locked in his father's truck with a total stranger. She holds a clipboard with a driver's exam rubric on it. She has a pen in her hand and a very serious looking pinstripe blouse with her name tag in all caps reading "LAILA."

"Yep. Newly minted sixteen-year-old here." Jamie sits in the driver's seat that he's sat in many times before. So many times that, frankly, the wear on the driver's seat might as well be attributed to him now. At least a quarter of the wear. Hogan could be responsible for the other quarter and his father for the rest. "Are we starting now?"

"Yes," says Laila. She tugs on her seatbelt to make sure it's snug and pulls her sunglasses over her eyes. "In case of Sun glare," she explains. "Now, what's the first thing you should do before driving?" Great. The questions have begun.

"Buckle up." Jamie looks down at his own seat belt. Check. "Turn on the engine." He twists his father's keys in the ignition and watches as Laila jumps a little in her seat. Twist-start engines probably aren't too common anymore. She's watching a historical demonstration at this point. "Check my mirrors, and if all looks good I can start driving, right?" Jamie glances in his side mirrors, which he adjusted before driving himself and his father to the Department of Motor and Electric Vehicles this morning.

He looks in the rearview mirror, and Laila confirms, "Yes, that's everything." Then she adds, "now, you'll back out slowly and drive to the edge of the parking lot, by that bar and grill at the edge of the shopping center. Take a right at that exit." Laila guides Jamie out of the parking lot, and Jamie pays close attention to her instructions for the next thirty minutes. By the end of it, Laila's quizzed him on hazards, letting blind folks cross the street, parking with the emergency brake while downhill, changing lanes, and guided Jamie back to the very parking lot in which they began. They park, and Laila unbuckles her seatbelt, ready to let herself out.

She hands a tablet to Jamie. "Here's the written portion of your exam." She jumps out of the truck. "Please follow me to our testing center." Jamie nods, holds the tablet, and follows her as she struts across the parking lot. A line wraps around the DMAEV building and they walk right past and into the building to a large room with countertops along the walls and screen dividers erected every three feet. "There are

30 questions and you have 2 hours to complete it. Of course, the sooner you finish, the sooner you can get on with your day. The tablet's in airplane mode, so no surfing the web for answers, and it's monitored by virtual proctors for cheating. Once you're done, you'll be given your results. If you pass the written exam, your driver's license will automatically be printed at your testing station and you can take it with you and go home. Good luck." Laila points to a compact printer fixed to the underside of the countertop before she turns and walks away.

Forty minutes later, Jamie walks out of the DMAEV with a freshly printed license in hand. As he exits the building, he scans the parking lot for Lance and his truck. Laila was supposed to return the keys to Jamie's legal guardian after the driving exam. When he spots his father, Jamie feigns sadness and walks to the passenger side door. He opens the door and lifts himself onto the passenger seat. Lance turns to Jamie, his expression neutral.

"How'd it go, son?"

"Not today," says Jamie.

"Hey, that's alright. Plenty of time to practice more." Lance reaches for Jamie's hand and squeezes it. "You're still the second best driver in our household." Jamie holds in a smile.

"Oh, sure," Jamie replies, milking it. "I'm not looking forward to what Hogan has to say about it. Or having to show up at school in my brother's ride still. Or be dropped off by my parents all year when the other juniors surely won't be."

"Tell you what, son. When you pass, cause you'll try again and you will, you can drive my truck to school for the first month." Lance smiles tenderly at Jamie. "Then you need to get a job and save up for your own daily drive." He pats Jamie's knee and twists his key in the ignition.

"Mean it?"

"Yeah, son." Jamie smiles. "Hm. Why are you looking at me like that? Did I just get tricked?" Jamie continues to smile and pulls his license from the pocket of his joggers.

"We'll, you're right. Took some time, but I passed." Lance pulls his son in for a hug.

"Can we revisit that promise I made you?" Jamie shakes his head. "Oh, fine. I was always going to let you borrow the truck anyway."

Jamie likes listening to *Clare and Jare In The Mornings* before driving to school. He wakes up, hops in the shower, and commands his virtual assistant to play FM 98.8 through his shower speakers. Then he heats up some French toast sticks from the freezer, eats, and hops in the car. Hogan is a senior and has a later start time than he does, so he can't count on him for a ride most days. All the more reason Jamie is glad to have acquired his own slice of adulthood by passing his driver's exam.

He hardly knows what market analysis is yet, but he likes Clare and Jare's banter and recognizes some companies and current events when they report on them. He is about to be a junior, and he is learning the ropes of how to talk like a man. Like Hogan.

The water is hot on his skin when he jumps in the shower this morning. "Paul, turn the temperature down 2 degrees." The virtual assistant takes the steps necessary to bring the shower from Scalding to Just Right. Beyond the sound of water falling on tile comes the sound of FM radio. Slight static. *Perfect.*

"Hello and welcome to Tuesday. This is Jare with *Clare and Jare In The Mornings*. I'm here with my prettier and more eloquent half, Clare Bagshaw, who has a market update for all our stock junkies out there." Jamie waves his hand in front of the soap dispenser, and soap falls into his palm. He rubs his palms together, lifts one arm at a time, and lathers.

"Thank you, Jare, and good morning listeners. Investors are acting on their enthusiasm for AI technologies and OVVL is up +6% after market open today, Thursday, August 29, 2030. Although today's gains indicate market recovery, Ovvl and its competitors in the AI Sector have seen stock volatility in recent weeks. The Intelligence Revolution may be creating a societal rift. While today's gains tell a different story, we have been seeing investors pull back and buy in and pull back and buy back in again week after week. Two weeks ago, OVVL stock was down -7.9%, after negative press surrounding one of the lawsuits in which the company is a defendant."

Water continues to fall on the tiled shower floor in large droplets. When Jamie decides he is sufficiently clean, he steps out of the shower with the water still running. "Paul, water off." The sound of water falling on tile ceases as Jamie walks out of his bathroom with a towel wrapped around his waist. "Paul, transfer audio to glasses."

Jamie absentmindedly grabs clothes from his closet and dons them, grabs his glasses off their stand, and heads downstairs. He pulls French toast sticks from the freezer, heats them in the toaster, and then sits at the kitchen table listening intently to the rest of the morning's hour segment of *Clare and Jare In The Mornings*. His fork cuts into French toast sticks sopping in syrup. As he brings each bite to his lips, he glances at the digital clock on the smart stove.

"A young filmmaker is suing Ovvl because of the terms of use for Whoot, one of Ovvl's popular chatbots, that he used while making an award-winning film, which premiered at this year's Sunny Plains Film Festival, the rights to which have been purchased for $5,000,000. Because the filmmaker used Whoot while developing the film, and because, pursuant to Whoot's terms of use, all creative works or businesses developed with the ideas generated by Whoot belong to Ovvl, it is Ovvl that is entitled to the profits. The filmmaker asserts in the lawsuit that the Whoot terms of use are unconscionable and that, because the nature of the work is creative, the ultimate expression of the film could not reasonably or primarily be attributed to Whoot."

"Well, this is certainly another one of many interesting court cases relating to the use of chatbots and creative expression," says Jare.

"Absolutely, Jare. And what makes this case even more intriguing than some of the previous cases we've discussed is that this filmmaker is a minor. Of course, the filmmaker's legal guardian is named as a Co-Plaintiff in the action, but legal complexity is introduced when the court considers the issue of his standing and whether he was breaching any terms of use due to his age at the time of use."

"I'm sure you will inform me and the listeners of any breaking news surround this lawsuit. When is the trial set to begin?"

"We expect the judge in the case to announce a formal trial date pending Ovvl's next answer," says Clare. Jamie chews his French toast and glances again at the time on the smart stove. 8:07 am.

"Paul, pause audio." Jamie grabs his bookbag and heads for his father's truck to drive himself to school.

Eight days later, Jamie is five minutes late to first period. Ms. Hart, Jamie's sophomore year English teacher is now his junior year English teacher too. She is in the middle of a sentence, and Jamie's appearance through the door doesn't disturb her flow in the slightest. Some of his peers who made it to class on time are no more present in this minute than Jamie was five minutes ago. Their heads, tucked inside soft hoodie jackets, rest on their palms and already their eyelids flutter closed and open and closed and open. 8:00 a.m. is no good to teenagers in any generation. Especially on Fridays. Jamie quietly takes his seat, dislodging his backpack from his shoulder.

"*Fahrenheit 451*, class. That's our next assigned reading." Ms. Hart walks across the front of the classroom containing approximately thirty teenage bodies. "As you read the words of Bradbury, I want you to consider what resemblance, if any, his words have to our world today." She holds a paperback book in her hand and lifts it up in front of the room. She taps the cover with her violet nails. Ms. Hart is always wearing red, or pink, or purple to match the whiteboard markers she uses. Behind her, violet letters on the whiteboard read: Intelligence Revolution, Conscious Choice, and Humanity. "And you will *read* this.

Despite being in the middle of an Intelligence Revolution, for the time being, our educational institutions are still focused on reading comprehension." *Intelligence Revolution.* Jamie's ears prick up at the phrase. Clare Bagshaw used this phrase approximately a week ago on *Clare and Jare In The Mornings.* "Unless you have received a waiver from the Principal for oral comprehension in place of reading comprehension, I expect each of you to check out a copy from our library. We'll walk there at the end of class so you can pick up a hardcopy or check out an e-reader." Ms. Hart turns her eyes to Jamie and nods in acknowledgement of his presence.

Intelligence Revolution. Jamie thinks to himself. What does that imply about human intelligence? Its past and its future?

"Class, search your tablets for this morning's group reading and get in your discussion groups. We'll have a class discussion in 30 minutes." Ms. Hart lets the teenagers self-organize and sits down behind her single monitor. She drowns out the presence of the tired juniors as she begins typing on her keyboard and getting lost in whatever it is English teachers type into search engines or word processors during class time.

Jamie remains in his chair as Beth, Yanet, and Kaleb pull back the chairs at his table to join him. This is their usual discussion group and will be for the entire trimester. Jamie pulls out the tablet hidden beneath the desk and his left hand begins swiping and typing across the screen in search of the morning's reading. *Ah, there it is.* A document cleanly titled "Friday Fiction" populates the tablet screen. Ms. Hart and her obvious naming conventions. Beth, Yanet, and Kaleb all catch each other's eyes as they pull up the reading on their own tablets.

Jamie's eyes track over the words on the screen.

A Boy's Wishes
By Edmund Yamato

All Jeremey wished for in his short life was one sentence from his father. Most children hold in their minds or their old birthday cards, minimally, one sentence from their father. If a child doesn't have one sentence in their minds or scrawled on their old birthday cards from their father, usually, they can knock on his bedroom door and ask him to write something down for their keeping. And your average father would either do just that or else yell about why he couldn't or wouldn't and then their children would minimally have one sentence in their minds.

But Jeremey had no "conventional" family; whatever that was supposed to mean, he didn't know. He only knew he had no bedroom door to knock on but for his mother's. And when he did knock on his mother's door as a young boy to ask where his father was, she would say, honestly, "I don't know, but I'm your mother, and I'm right here."

When he was old enough to know the alphabet and write to Santa Claus, he used to wish for Santa to find his father and bring him home for Christmas. His mother read his letters before mailing them to Santa, of course, and for some reason Santa stopped writing back to him about his wishes at Christmas time. Which was strange, since Santa usually took the time to write all the kids on his Nice list, and his mother told him he made it on the Nice list by a narrow margin every year.

So he stopped wishing to find his father and started wishing he could have the best clothes, the best shoes, the best toys. If he couldn't have a father and a whole family to belong to like all his classmates at school, he could at least be the kid who had the best. Who all the other kids wanted to play with. He could at least belong with them. And then Santa wrote to him to explain he was asking for quite a lot, and all the other kids on the Nice list needed some things as well. Would he consider sharing?

Later, when Jeremy found out Santa wasn't real, that it was his mother who couldn't grant his wish to find his father, that wouldn't downright spoil him to make up for his perceived lack, he wished he were enough. He was so afraid he wasn't.

This fear reminded Jeremy of when he was a child, somewhere around five years old. He used to ask his mother to tell him the story of how she met his father. He used to ask her if he had his father's eyes. If his father liked cartoons and cereal for dinner like he did. When he was a growing boy, somewhere around eleven or so, he used to ask her if his father was tall. He wanted to know if he could expect growth spurts. He asked her if his father played any sports. If his father preferred music or drawing instead. And when he was a teenager, around seventeen thereabouts, he stopped asking his mother questions about him altogether. He was just "him" now. He wasn't his father. He hadn't been his father nearly his whole life. He realized all "he" ever was the means to Jeremy's own existence. And all "he" would ever be to Jeremy was one part of a mathematical formula.

A very necessary part of the mathematical equation where one plus one equals three. Jeremy's mother grew up when doctors were beginning to find that fertility among women was declining. Not many women were having children anymore; certainly, not in large quantities. Women had never been property to breed, but now they weren't treated like they were, and they quite liked working, earning a living, and creating careers for themselves.

The few women who did choose to have children found it biologically hard to have any. Like Jeremy's mom. "I knew I always wanted you, Jer," his mother used to tell him. "Every water fountain I saw, I'd toss a coin in, and I'd wish for you. There was this one fountain in the courtyard of the apartments I lived in during my late twenties. A sculpture of a fish was in the middle. The fish was jumping up, toward the sky, and from its lips spout the water. The bath below it was covered in coins, some silver, but mostly copper, lucky pennies..."

The story goes on for five pages. Jamie looks up and around the table when he finishes reading. Beth has finished as well and is now drawing cartoons in the margins of their reading with her stylus. Jamie has caught her doing this a few times before. The stylus isn't school issue. It's pink and has small rhinestones along the side. Jamie sees how Kaleb looks at her when she uses that pink stylus of hers. Kaleb finds it endearing. Jamie imagines feeling that way about someone. He'd like to find that too.

Kaleb and Yanet put their tablets flat on the desk. "Well, damn, wasn't expecting to read about our birth rate crisis this morning," says Yanet, who is finished with reading as well.

Beth blushes from across the table. "Right? A poignant topic for our days. You think they're trying to tell us teenagers something?"

"That would be real cheeky of the school administration. Especially after all the your body your choice legislation here in California the past ten years," says Yanet.

The boys sit and listen, waiting for their opinions to be asked for. "Right," says Beth. She tucks a strand of her dyed blonde hair behind her ear. "So, aside from the allusion to the natality issue, what did you think about the idea of wishes?"

"Mm, it was kind of an interesting frame for the reader to explore the gratitude they feel for what they *do* have. Or maybe an interesting frame for exploring the different perspectives of what having a father could mean. Like, one kid could have a great dad who writes stuff down for them when their kid asks them to, and one could have a crappy dad who yells at their kid for asking anything of them, and both of these types of dads could be great to a third kid who doesn't have a dad at all. Y'know?"

"Yeah, totally. That's a great point, Kaleb. Really strange, in a good way, how that third perspective comes in from out of nowhere too. Almost like the piece is set up to create a false dichotomy. And then the narrator just tears into it," says Beth. She smiles at Kaleb as she fiddles with the pink stylus in her hands.

"Yeah," Jamie joins in. "I liked that bit too. I also think the narrator might be trying to convey that there are three types of wishes. And one type is our species' optimistic attempt to erase the worst-case scenario."

"Lot of words there, Harken," says Beth. For some reason unknown to Jamie, Beth insists on calling him by his last name. Jamie's only guess aside from her wanting to irritate him is that she was raised in a military home. "Want to break it down a little slower? What are the other two types of wishes?"

"Hey, not everyone here is slow, Beth," says Kaleb with what Jamie detects as a hint of flirtation in his voice, if Jamie is reading the room right. Beth now blushes from across the table.

"Sure," says Jamie. He stuffs his hands in the pocket of his jacket and leans back in his chair. "First, let me ask, what do you make a wish for?"

"How do you mean?" Asks Beth.

"I mean, why do you wish in the first place? Why does anyone decide to say, 'Hey, Universe. I wish for,'" Jamie flicks his wrist, "whatever?"

"Um, because a person wants something?"

"Yep. I agree. All wishes are due to wanting. But we *want*, I think, generally three different things. So why does a person *want* that something?"

"Because they do? I don't know, Harken, isn't that an it-depends kind of thing? You haven't gotten real specific."

"Sure, it can depend. Let's run with a wish for super-human speed. Why would someone wish for super-human speed? Why would they *want* it?"

"Because it would be hella cool," says Kaleb. "For one. And then they wouldn't be slow. They're trading being slow for being super-human fast. Way better option, frankly."

"So is that greedy? Is that innocent? Why would someone not want to be slow?"

"Could be it's a disadvantage to be slow. Quick reflexes can really save a person in a tricky situation. Or can help you save someone else in a tricky situation," says Yanet.

"So that wish could be greedy if we just want super-human speed to be cool or that wish could be innocent if we want super-human speed to help others. What's the worst thing that could happen if we're slow?"

"Well, your uncle could get stabbed by a robber if you're not fast enough to stop him," says Kaleb. "That would be a pretty worst-case scenario."

"Yeah. You might not stop an intruder in your house from getting to your kiddos," says Yanet. Her eyes stare down toward the floor. Yanet doesn't have kiddos yet. But what she does have is an active imagination. No wonder she runs track.

"Yes, great examples. Those are pretty worst-case scenarios. And scary. But if someone had super-human speed, those scenarios wouldn't exist at all, would they? Those fears would basically be nullified. Right?"

"Guess so, Harken," says Beth. She says this with an air of *bored* about her. "What's your point?"

"I think we wish because we want something either innocently, greedily, or out of fear. What good does it do us to nullify the worst-case scenario?"

"We don't have to fear," says Kaleb. "We're not afraid of the worst-case scenario any more because it doesn't exist," he says.

"Exactly. And all that you have left is hope. No fear. You begin seeing only the good possibilities."

"When in other times all you would have seen are the bad ones," echoes Kaleb.

"Okay, so what does that say about our protagonist though?" asks Beth.

"Well, his first wish was pretty innocent. He just wanted Santa to bring his father home. And his second, for cool clothes and shoes, was greedier in comparison. Although I'm not sure greed is the right word to describe Jeremy's motivation here. Anyway, then he just wanted to be enough because he feared he wasn't, yeah?" Yanet pieces their group's discussion together with the text.

"Okay, I see," says Beth, biting her stylus. "We can make a bunch of types of wishes. But two types, innocent wishes and greedy wishes, we gain something from and the other we lose something from. Like we could gain health or money but lose our fear."

"Said another way," says Kaleb, "we always think we gain something from innocent or greedy wishes but we always get hope from the third."

"Oh man," comments Yanet. "Then what's the line between hope and fear?"

The ceiling of Jamie's bedroom only grows more fascinating with the passing of days and creeping up of the fall equinox. The sunlight is pristine around four in the afternoon, which happily turns out to be when Jamie arrives home from school. He pulls his father's truck into the driveway and begins to head upstairs to his bedroom. Time to lay there, stare, and lose himself.

Jamie removes his shoes when he enters the house, placing the ball of one foot on the heel of his other and pulling one foot out of one shoe followed by the other. His father walks down the hallway. "Jamie?" He calls.

"Yeah, Dad. It's me."

"Oh good." Lance stands near the staircase, taking in the sight of his son turning into a young man. In his hand, Lance holds a hot cup of coffee he must have just asked Paul to pour. Steam still rises from the cup and his fingers curl around the mug's handle. He takes a sip and then winces, wishing he had thought better of it. "What'd they teach you today?" Lance never asks a question just to ask it. He wants the answer.

"Ms. Hart taught my English class first period. My teacher last year. She had us read this fiction piece about fathers, wishes, and natality. The protagonist was an *in vitro fertilization* baby whose mother used a sperm donor to have him. The protagonist was really upset he didn't have a dad in the traditional sense."

"Oh." Lance shifts his weight from one foot to the other. "That's a different take. What did you think about the story?"

"Eh, not something I would read on my own."

"But?"

"But I guess I'm looking forward to our new reading assignment." Lance's eyebrows perk up at this statement by Jamie. "I know. Ms. Hart is a good teacher. You'd like her. She's a little old school too." Lance purses his lips and smiles.

"Yeah, I met her at least year's parent-teacher conferences. Smart cookie. So tell me about this new reading assignment you're excited about."

"Well, it's reading Ray Bradbury's *Fahrenheit 451.* You ever read that in school?" Lance nods, a sly smile creeping across his face. "Yeah, so it's supposed to be one of those 1950s dystopian novels. The synopsis makes it sound super censorship oriented. Kind of resembles our perception of China, but Ms. Hart thinks it's also telling of the Intelligence Revolution we're in."

"The intelligence revolution we're in?"

"Yeah," Jamie pauses. He is certain Ms. Hart said more than simply allege some revolution exists. But now his mind won't permit him to remember the details. "Sounds like it'll be part of our class discussion."

"Sounds ominous," says Lance, finally deciding to hazard another sip of his coffee.

No grimace passes across his face this time. "Keep me informed?"

"Sure," Jamie nods. "Hey, where's Hogan?"

"Oh, I think he's upstairs listening to more of that garbage." His father waives his free hand about next to his head like he's swatting off a fly. Jamie nods again. Must be Brad Rayne back at it with the AI or Bye slogan. Jamie is growing worried. He'd heard whispers at school about seniors planning to run away to tech-heavy cities to get away from their restrictive, luddite parents. "Ludds," they call such parents. And the cities are called "Upgrowth Cities." They're cities that plan to lower the age of majority to permit young adults, meaning seventeen-year-olds who felt eighteen, to consent to their own BCI surgeries when their parents otherwise wouldn't.

"Okay, might ask for his help if he's had Ms. Hart before."

"Don't bother. If your brother was assigned that book, he wouldn't have read it."

"But the participation and essay response are half the class grade -"

"- that wouldn't have mattered much to him."

And Jamie hesitates to admit it, but he knows his father is probably right. Hogan denounced 1950s dystopian novels. *Educational institutions and parents like to use all those "what ifs" those novels pose to control their kids' behavior, Jamie. They're not used to the technology we're used to. It's a strange new world to them but a totally natural thing for the world to change. And I guess a human thing to reject change. But yeah. It's a bunch of fear mongering; screw those old books.* Hogan's voice comes to Jamie from the ether, although it's been a while since he actually talked to his brother at length.

"Okay. Well thanks, Dad. Good to see you." And with that, Jamie struts up the stairs with his backpack hanging off one shoulder.

Of course, Jamie was a reasonably smart boy, and he figured the phrase "Intelligence Revolution" surely had something to do with the plethora of smart technologies engulfing daily life. He figured Paul was a good example of this, and Doorman David, and the far too straight-faced, intelligently generated evening news anchor, and the self-driving cars his father expressly didn't trust. Three decades ago, assistants were hired and sometimes had affairs that ripped families apart, not simply pocket computers who constantly eavesdrop and blindly listen to a person's commands to set 50 timers at once. Doormen primarily existed in New York City and belonged only to the very wealthy for a hefty hourly wage, not simply for anyone who could pay a monthly subscription on credit. News stations had several flesh newscasters competing against each other for the title of anchor. And cars used to involve your feet as much as your hands. At least this is what Jamie's two most credible sources, his father and his father's favorite movies, told and showed him. So obviously technology was becoming intelligent. But exactly what did Clare mean when she said this was a revolution in her sly, Clareish undertone? What did Ms. Hart mean when she wrote it on the whiteboard?

Now that he thought about it, Jamie is surprised it wasn't his history teacher, Mr. Briggs, who mentioned this revolution to him first. He could easily make the voice of Mr. Briggs commentate in his head about the Intelligence Revolution. *How interesting is it, Class, when we juxtapose our current cultural moment with artificial intelligence against the Industrial Revolution or the Agricultural Revolution?* Although, Jamie supposed, the Intelligence Revolution was in the midst of unraveling. If it hadn't yet concluded, it couldn't be formal history yet.

Later, Jamie would realize it was 2030 and cartoon shows had been projecting science would have come way farther than Brain Computer Interfaces by now. We were supposed to have colonized Mars by now. And although we hadn't, it certainly wasn't more than ten years out. Ovvl's announcement that BCIs were coming to market really wasn't all that unforeseen.

But to Lance, Hogan, and many others, this announcement began a ripple through American society. Jamie could now distill it down to that moment in his father's F150 listening to *Clare and Jare In The Mornings* announce Ovvl's big news – that was the moment that his society shifted, or rather fractured, into accepting artificial intelligence or refusing to. And looking around, those that rejected AI did so either due to financial unaffordability, personal values, or both. Those that accepted AI were probably overconfident and driven by the human ego's need to explore its own invention.

The first trimester of Hogan's senior year wasn't even over when he left. Sometime between Thanksgiving break and Christmas, Hogan disappeared.

Jamie was the last one in his family to see Hogan. It was a Saturday, which seemed to Jamie like one of the least suspicious days because Hogan would naturally be out almost all night long with one or another of his enigmatic friends. And that's where he was off to, actually, when Jamie caught him sifting about his bedroom.

"Hey, Hoag. If I wanted to find the best virtual reality cafe to take a girl to on a first date –" Jamie leans against the side of the doorframe to Hogan's bedroom. He stiffens when he realizes Hogan is ignoring him, and not just ignoring him because he's thinking, but because he is calculatedly packing. A black hardshell suitcase lays open on his bed. Hogan places items neatly into it, folds and refolds, stacks and restacks items he likes wearing or hanging up on his wall. Items Hogan likes way too much to lock away in some hardshell suitcase in his closet. No. He is leaving. "What are you doing, Hogan?" Jamie asks. Hogan looks up and his face pales. Like he's been caught.

"Obviously, packing."

"Okay. Why are you packing?"

"I need to go, Jamie. This isn't the home I need."

"What do you mean this isn't the home you need? You don't really get to pick your family."

"You'll learn soon enough that you do. And I need a home that lets me explore my interests and won't hold me back in the twentieth century."

"It's not the twentieth century, Hoag."

"Ah, there you're right. It's almost the twenty second. But Mom and Dad won't accept that, Ludds they are."

"Mom's not a Ludd, Hoag. I'm sure she could convince Dad if that's what this is all about. If you want more freedom with the virtualverse permissions at home or something, just tell her. It's not like they force a curfew or many rules on you, you know."

"That's not the issue, Jamie." Hogan continues walking back and forth between the suitcase on his bed, his closet, and his desk. He continues grabbing items, folding them or sorting them, and placing them gently into the suitcase. "The issue is Mom and Dad are afraid of change. We're entering a whole new era and they're not going to adapt well. I want to adapt well. I can learn. But if they're not open minded, it's going to hold back my growth. I can't let that happen." Jamie stands in the doorway, feeling sympathetic for his brother.

"To be fair, I'm afraid of change too."

"Yeah, but the difference with you, Jamie, is that this is your era. This is your generation. You were born into this. It'll be easy for you to adapt. Just like me. You probably don't think twice about a lot of our technology. Unless Dad's gotten to you and planted little seeds of doubt." Jamie swallows. He does consider his father's perspective informative. Although sometimes outdated.

"Yeah, maybe."

Hogan looks up at Jamie and asks, "Don't you want to leave too?" His green eyes hold Jamie's brown. He's not mocking Jamie. He's genuinely asking. "I know my friend's ride is going to be tight tonight, but I'm sure we could double up." Hogan searches Jamie's face for some kind of response. "We're going to one of those Upgrowth Cities. Don't know which one yet."

Jamie is surprised. To see his brother preparing to leave his family. To leave him. To have planned this out for so long, clearly. And Jamie thinks of his parents finding out their first born ran away. And he thinks about his parents finding out both their sons ran away. And he pictures his father making his coffee too hot and trying to drink it, and listening to the radio in his truck, and sitting in his recliner doing nothing but sit, and he doesn't feel right about saying yes to Hogan's proposal. He belongs here. He doesn't want his life to change that drastically. He wants to come home to his bed and drive his father's truck to school and eat his mother's cooking and have Paul play *Clare and Jare In The Mornings* while he showers and finishes Ms. Hart's English class. And he wants to take a girl on a first date like he came up here to ask about.

"So?" Asks Hogan, zipping his suitcase up.

"I can't."

"You mean you won't." Hogan hauls the suitcase off his bed and quietly, delicately, places it on the floor. "And that's okay, little brother." Jamie winces. He's almost as grown up as Hogan is now. "You stay where you belong." Jamie's chest feels like a war zone. His heart is pumping fast and his hands are sweating and he wants to cry maybe. To Jamie's ears it sounds like Hogan just said Jamie doesn't belong with him.

And the last he saw of his brother was his silhouette darting out from the garage later that night and into one of his friend's self driving cars with his black suitcase in tow.

"**H**ogan leaving feels personal as hell. But, son, mark my words, it's not personal at all. This phenomenon of youth leaving their families is not unique to us – we're going to see plenty of it. This Intelligence Revolution is going to make us choose sides. And Hogan's just chosen to be on the artificial side of it." Lance stares at his son. The only one left living under his roof that is.

Deanna hadn't come home yet. Lance avoids walking near the phone. If his father calls his mother and tells her their eldest son ran away, would that make reality feel more real? Would that make Deanna pick a side in the revolution?

Jamie didn't see all the days his brother left his bedroom door shut for what they were. He assumed Hogan was being a young adult. He assumed Hogan was making his own space. He assumed Hogan wanted privacy to do as young men pleased. He didn't see the shut door as a door closing on his family. But Jamie remembered the voices behind the closed door. He remembered the hot rhetoric his brother consumed.

Maybe it was obvious all along that Hogan was slipping away. All of the times Hogan turned down playing in the virtualverse with Jamie. All of the times he lacked enthusiam to climb trees in their neighborhood to yell "penis!" at neighbors walking by with their wireless headphones stuffed in their ears. All of the times Hogan skipped class and rode away in one of his tech savvy friends' self-driving cars. All of the times Hogan refused to bite his tongue around their father and called him a Ludd.

Things changed quickly for the Harkens after that. And for the world.

"No! No. Lance, I don't see why moving is necessary," says Deanna. "This is the world we're in! Welcome to it! It's different than when we grew up. I get that it's upsetting. But you just aren't living in reality, honey -"

"- But I am, Dee. I am the only one living in reality. I figured if anyone could see what's wrong with where we're headed, it would be you." Lance says in the calmest voice he can manage to Deanna. To his wife.

"Oh, don't you dare put that on me, Lance: the responsibility to see what's wrong with the world, what you think is wrong with the world, and rectify it."

"I'm not asking you to rectify it, Dee. I'm just saying that you always had your head in both worlds. You have always been so good at holding the ugly and the beautiful in the same field of view. You know the ugly side of AI as well as you know the beautiful side of it."

"Maybe when it comes to art, sweetheart, but this is life we're talking about and this technology is just part of our lives now. It's neither ugly nor beautiful. It just is. Leave it be."

"Hey, it was you who insisted we enroll our children in public schools with teachers who had experience teaching before this mid-century chaos. You didn't want to simply leave it be then. You didn't want to chance their education and critical thought in an economically and technologically disruptive environment then."

"Sure, but I didn't expect that enrolling them in public schools without excessive technological resources and with capable teachers would entirely keep our children from the technology of today's age. And it didn't. They have tablets in their classrooms now just like the kids in those magnet schools. I just thought it would teach them to think a little harder."

"I think you need to do a little of that right now, Dee."

"Excuse me?"

"Think about Hogan. He's long gone. Off to New York or someplace with the lifestyle he covets. Some place that'll let him consent to his own brain surgery at seventeen. Dee, he isn't the only teen to do this. Our society is fracturing, okay? One day, we'll wake up and half our population will be gone."

"Listen to yourself. That's exactly what you're asking me to do."

"What?"

"Run off, away with you, to some new development that's entirely comfortable living in a fractured society and without the advances we should be forced to adapt to. Together. Gosh, grow up, Lance."

Lance shakes his head. "It's going to happen anyway, Dee."

"What is?"

"This societal fracturing. I mean, it became inevitable the second Ovvl brought BCIs to the scene. Only a select few are going to be able to afford that kind of technology. And of those that can afford it, some are going to reject it for being outside their values. What we're faced with now is choosing a life of convenience or a life of humanity."

"Can't we afford it?"

Lance frowns. His wife is missing the point.

"You're upset you've been out of work so long, Lance. I get it. But we can afford it. And even if we couldn't, so many companies are committed to offering AI courses for free to help solve the inevitable inequities this technology will introduce. Naturally, you're mad at this mid-century lifestyle. I get it. It robbed you of work you were good at. But are you really going to let it rob you of enjoying life?"

"First of all, that's not fair," Lance begins to say. "Losing work isn't why I feel this way."

"We could be with Hogan you know. He only left us because he thinks we're not going to adapt well to this new age."

"I see," says Lance simply.

"So what's the big hold up?"

"You're not the woman I married anymore."

Deanna's mouth freezes. Her jaw is open, ready to speak, but her lips quiver. Her hands quiver too. Finally, she replies, "Well." And then she gathers her purse from the entry way table and lets herself out without another word.

A person usually spends quite some time picking up and rearranging the pieces of their fractured life when their world falls apart. Following such a period, a person often finds themselves in a wholly new form. Arranged from the same pieces but in an entirely new order, perhaps missing a piece or two, perhaps composed of smaller, new pieces that resulted from the breaking apart of larger, old ones.

The fragmenting of Jamie's world looked like this: first, his father lost his job; second, his brother ran away from home; third, his mother left too; fourth, Ovvl forced everyone to assimilate or be left behind; fifth, Jamie and Lance decided to leave the evolving world behind.

"Jamie," Lance stands in the dark kitchen of their family's home. Only Lance and Jamie have been inhabiting it the last two months. "I found a new borough in Arizona. Intelligence Revolution antagonists have been moving there. Want to go with me? We can drive out there."

Jamie sits on the couch in the darkness. He's been sitting there in the darkness each evening since his mother left. No more staring at the ceiling in his bedroom while golden light filtered in. This period of his life lacked the feeling of golden hour. And, beyond that, Jamie and his father couldn't practically afford light. Deanna was the remaining one of his parents with a job. And now she didn't come home. And his father wanted to save money while he was figuring out his next move, so they kept the lights off. Less light. Less bills. Less hope. Jamie wished he were born in an earlier era. He wished the geniuses in the world knew what they were doing when they made AI. He wished it wasn't true that the only constant is change. He feared living in the mid-century with all its uncertainty. He feared AI may not be able to be controlled, and if it was, he feared it was the ultimate evolution of humanity. He feared that the only constant is change.

"Okay. I'll go with you. Why Arizona though? Why can't we stay here in Encinitas?"

A look of relief crosses over Lance's face. Probably because he won't be alone. He'll have some family to still belong to. "Too many folks too comfortable with AI are moving out here. You know, the very well to do who are pocketing millions from AI. Won't be a very mixed population soon." By mixed population, his father meant AI protagonists and AI antagonists.

"Then we'll be with our antagonistic peers soon enough. When are we leaving?"

Now, Jamie is thirty-two years and four months old. His son just entered the world. *Oliver*, he and his wife, Penny, named him. A child born into a world full of twists. A world with prosperity but without peace.

Years have passed since Lance and Jamie moved to their borough in Arizona. Roughly sixteen, although Jamie could swear those sixteen years held twenty or thirty years of life within them. Lance was all the family Jamie had until he met Penny. Now he has Lance, Penny, and Oliver too.

Jamie sits up in bed with the bedside lamp on. Penny lays on her side next to him. Her black hair is trimmed just above her shoulders and her bangs fall on her forehead in a tousled manner. Their son, Oliver, lays on his back between the two of them. His little hands extend above him, reaching out for nothing in particular but the texture of the world beyond that he hadn't yet the full capacity to take in. His little feet kick every now and then, and Penny tickles his tummy with her index finger, which causes Oliver to emit faint gurgles and giggles. He's three months old.

"I thought I saw Hogan on the news the other day," Penny says.

"Was it?"

"No, I don't think so. They referred to him as a Mr. Harken, but he didn't look anything like the boy in the photos you showed me."

"Why was he on the news?"

"They were reporting on another case of brain hacking. Mr. Harken is apparently the executive of a large nuclear energy company, and some bad actors were able to get into his Brain Computer Interface while it was turned on and siphoned off millions from his personal bank accounts. The authorities are tracking the transactions to see if the sum is recoverable or has been used for illicit purposes already."

Jamie's eyes widen. What if it was Hogan? "Where did this happen?" Jamie doesn't know where Hogan ran away to, but he can't help asking.

"New York." Penny tickles Ollie's tummy again and the three-month-old laughs again.

"This is the third hacking this year. Makes me glad we chose as we did. Strange to think our bodies could be controlled like that. Almost like controlling our thoughts."

"I guess. Although, given the number of BCIs in use, you'd think there would be a lot more than three incidents."

"Maybe famous executives over index as victims of that particular crime. There are probably more cases that aren't reported or are handled privately or aren't as high stakes or involve everyday people."

"What did he look like? The man on the news?"

"Oh, blonde, not very tall. His beard was tinted orange a little."

Penny is right. Doesn't sound like Hogan. "What color were his eyes?"

"I couldn't tell."

"You have a brother, Daddy?" Oliver asks as Jamie tucks his son into bed. This is the first time Oliver has asked him this question.

And, as many times as Jamie has tried to prepare himself to answer it, nothing comes to his mind as being right enough a response.

"I do."

"Why don't you tell me about him?" A tinge of remorse coats Oliver's question. A heavy emotion for a seven-year-old to carry for a decision he had no hand in making.

"Well, we don't see him very much," Jamie said carefully.

"Would you tell me about him? Please?" Oliver asks. And then he bites his little seven-year-old lip and fiddles with his little seven-year-old hands and says, "I haven't had a brother."

"Okay," says Jamie. "Okay, I can tell you about Uncle Hogan, Ollie." Jamie inhales and looks into his own memory to recall the face of a man he hadn't seen for twenty-three years. A man who was a boy the last time he saw him. Only two years older than he was. Jamie clears his throat and looks back at Oliver, who is laying patiently in his bed, green eyes fixed on Jamie's brown. "Years ago, son, people made a huge discovery:

computers and humans could become one. And this was exciting for some and daunting for others."

Young Oliver listens to his father speak intently. Oliver is tucked comfortably underneath a blue bedspread. His face is round, turned up to his father who is sitting beside him.

"Our brightest scientists made this discovery and it scared even some of them. Picture men and women in white lab coats. Or in jeans and black T-shirts because that's often what these type of scientists wore.

All of the computers in this borough we live in simply make calculations and process information based on rules that we programmed for them. But outside of this borough, in Upgrowth Cities, there are smart computers that recognize speech, can formulate natural language, and can create ideas. Granted, those smart computers still follow a set of rules programmed just for them. But they are smart like us, and think like us, and some even question like us. Our borough implements network security measures to ensure our computers don't interact or exchange information with the Upgrowth Cities' smart computers. We live in a select technology borough, and Uncle Hogan lives in an Upgrowth City somewhere. That's why we don't see him."

"How come we live so differently than the people in those cities?"

"Ollie, I'm not sure how much to say to you about all this. You're seven. I don't know how much you care about a world decades past."

"Hey. I'm seven. Why does that matter?" Ollie says in his typical, matter of fact way. His attitude and confidence bring a smile to Jamie's lips. But Jamie knows, as his parent, some things are less developmentally appropriate to tell Ollie at this age.

"Well, I guess you're right, mister. But this is my perspective. Maybe it isn't all as bad as I remember it. I don't want you thinking my opinion is the only way to think." Oliver throws the bedsheets off excitedly and scoots up against his pillows to sit up straight. He's wearing long-sleeved pajamas with a plaid print. Blue and green. Hogan's favorite color mixed with Jamie's. The hour is late, but Oliver's young childhood attention is captured. "I'll just try my best, son. Okay?"

"Uncle Hogan was naturally tech savvy. Like how you are savvy at reading your Mommy's old picture books and knowing exactly what voice to use for each character, Ollie. He certainly wasn't afraid of computers. We had them all over growing up, more than we do now. Little computers the size of half a peanut and butter jelly sandwich. You know these ones – phones. You can fit them in the palm of your hand and keep it in your pocket. We also had them in our eyeglasses. They were so tiny, you could fit the components into the sides of the glasses and the glasses manufacturers could add a screen into one of the lenses. We also had them in our walls to control the lights, the television, the phone and the music we wanted to listen to. We had laptops, like we do now, that we would keep on our desks or sometimes bring into bed or to different stores, like the coffee shop Mommy likes here. We had them in cars. Right in the front underneath the rearview mirror next to the driver's seat. Everywhere.

Uncle Hogan liked all of that. He liked smart computers especially because they could think. He thought, *What a cool feature*, rather than, *how terrifying.* A lot of people thought, *how terrifying.* He was smart too.

He built some computers. With his hands and lots of different tools. He was two years older than me. He loved the color blue. Everything in his room was blue," at this, Oliver beams. Everything in his room is blue too. "His eyes were green. He had black hair like me and Grandpa Lance. He was very pale because he hardly ever went outside. He was on the computer most of the time, so he had no reason to go see the Sun. His favorite subject in school was History and his second favorite was computer science. He and I used to climb trees together."

"Real ones?"

"Real ones." Ollie's eyes widen. This is the most he's ever heard of his Uncle, and he had no clue they climbed trees then too. "What else do you want to know?"

"Where is he now?" Ollie looks at Jamie earnestly. Ollie wonders, the way in which his father talks about his brother, he seems to have liked him. Why didn't they still speak? Why hadn't he met him?

"Oh, I don't know Ollie. That's the thing. He ran away from home when he was seventeen. He could have gone to New York, or Los Angeles, or Seattle, or San Francisco.

Again, he lives in some Upgrowth City somewhere. Any one of those big tech cities would have done well for him."

"He ran away from home? Why would he do that?"

"Oh yeah. He liked computers, like I said, and Grandpa Lance didn't really like how smart computers were becoming. So Uncle Hogan ran away to be with other people like him, who wanted computers to learn and thought smart computers could be good. He was an optimist, really."

"That's sad he ran away. I bet Grandpa misses him. What's an optimist?"

"Someone who sees the good as being better than the bad."

"Oh," Ollie nods. "So what was Grandpa then?"

"More of a pessimist."

"And a pessimist is what?"

"Someone who sees the bad as being more plentiful than the good."

"Oh, okay. So they didn't really agree. Grandpa and Uncle Hogan."

"Nope."

"And you didn't either, did you, Dad? You and Grandpa moved here together."

"That's right, Ollie. I wanted to believe in the good, like my brother. But it felt so important to get this choice right, whether to believe or not, and my father seemed like the voice of reason." Ollie nods, mulling this all over in his head. Jamie sits in silence for a moment with his son. He's grown so fast. And sometimes, his green eyes and sharp questions remind him of Hogan.

"You know how Grandpa Lance always asks questions and expects answers?" Ollie nods. Even he knew that at age seven.

"What I should have realized was that nobody has them. Not the AI protagonists and not the AI antagonists. We were all making the best decisions we thought we could make for ourselves based on the information we had at the time. Your Uncle Hogan made the best decision for himself. And I made the best decision for myself. I grew up with the same technology as Hogan, yet I heard my father's voice in the back of my mind and, to me, that always sounded like reason. Now I think, sometimes, it was fear."

"Thank you for telling me about Uncle Hogan." Ollie smiles. "I bet a smart computer could find him for you." Jamie considers this. He was sure it could too. But they didn't have those in their borough and it had been years since they last spoke. Plus, Jamie wouldn't necessarily want to find his way about an AI society. He was too used to this new normal they had built in his borough of select technologies handpicked by its constituents. The cities outside would be foreign places to navigate.

"Maybe, son." Jamie says.

"I'd like to meet him when you find him." Ollie wiggles himself back under his bedsheets. His eyes are finally fluttering closed. His head lays on the pillow comfortably, and the glow from his analog alarm clock illuminates the smile on his son's face.

"Me too," says Jamie, referring not just to his son meeting his brother but to himself meeting his brother again for the first time.

They were both new men now, surely, shaped by the fractured pieces of their pasts. "Me too."

ABOUT THE AUTHOR

Leigh Maris is foremost a reader of cereal boxes, product labels, and tables of contents. Secondarily, she is an author of short musings and forthcoming novels and hopes her words matter to at least one other person. She obtained her Bachelor's of Arts in English Rhetoric and Composition from California State University, Long Beach, where her favorite past times were bringing textbooks to the beach and drinking copious amounts of coffee that's mainly milk. To support Leigh is also to support the small, terribly cute border collie mix living with her, and, most importantly, your own word devouring habit.

Also by Leigh Maris

<u>Short Story</u>

Aquarians and Acquisitions

Our Place

Lucid

Synapse